D1395580

Published by Ladybird Books Ltd
80 Strand London WC2R 0RL
A Penguin Company
9 10

Printed in Italy

Disney

The SORCERER'S APPRENTICE

Ladybird

A grand orchestra had gathered. They were going to play a wonderful piece of music called *The Sorcerer's Apprentice*. It told an old story about a brilliant magician and his helper, who was once a little *too* helpful!

The musicians tuned their instruments as the conductor stepped up to his place and raised his baton ready to begin.

This was going to be an extra special performance. The story was going to be acted out and Mickey Mouse was going to play the part of the sorcerer's apprentice.

Suddenly, there was a hush in the theatre as the audience became quiet. The lights dimmed and the curtains rose. It was time for the story to begin…

Long, long ago there lived a sorcerer who knew everything there was to know about magic.

The sorcerer had a very tall, very special hat. Whenever he wore this hat, he could just *think* magic thoughts and they would come true.

The sorcerer could think about a butterfly and one would appear. But he would have to say secret magic words to make it disappear!

The wise sorcerer had a helper,
Mickey Mouse.

Mickey did all the work around the
sorcerer's castle. He swept the floor,
he chopped the wood and he carried
water from the fountain.

Mickey knew about the sorcerer's magic hat. "If only I had that hat!" he said. "I could just *think* about my work and it would be done. I would *never* have to work again!"

One day, the sorcerer had to go out. He left his hat on a table in the cellar, deep in the castle where Mickey was working. Mickey knew that this was his chance…

"Now *I* can be a great sorcerer!" he said, as he put the hat onto his head.

He looked around the cellar and
saw an old broom standing up
against the wall. "I'll start by putting
a spell on that broom," he said.

So Mickey did what the sorcerer always did. He thought magic thoughts and pointed his fingers at the broom.

All at once, the broom began to glow. Then it began to move…

"Broom, pick up the buckets!"
Mickey ordered.

The broom grew arms and did just
what Mickey had said.

"Follow me!" said Mickey, walking
up the steps that led out of the cellar.
The broom quickly marched up the
steps after him.

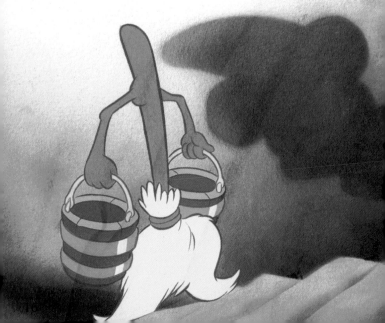

"Go to the fountain and fill the buckets with water," Mickey continued.

The broom filled the buckets.

Then, Mickey ordered the broom to carry the buckets back and pour the water into a well in the middle of the cellar. The broom did exactly as it was told.

Mickey laughed. "Magic is easy! I'll never have to work again!" he said as he sat down in the sorcerer's chair.

As Mickey watched the broom work, he began to yawn. Soon, he was fast asleep...

Mickey dreamt that he was the most powerful sorcerer in the whole world. He made the stars and the planets zoom through space. He sent comets flashing across the universe and made fantastic fireworks light up the sky.

Then, Mickey dreamt he ruled the oceans. He made the sea rise up in mighty waves.

But in Mickey's dream, the waves kept rising higher and higher, crashing all around him, until...

Suddenly, he woke up. To his surprise he found that he really *was* surrounded by water.

While Mickey had been dreaming, the broom had carried on working.

It hadn't stopped once the well was full. The broom had carried on tipping bucket after bucket of water into it. Now, the cellar was flooded!

Mickey leapt up. "Stop!" he cried.
"Stop, broom! Stop!"

But those were not the magic words
that would break the spell. The
broom did not stop! It carried on
fetching the water.

As Mickey chased after the broom,
he saw an axe. He grabbed it and
chopped the broom into hundreds
of tiny pieces.

"I've stopped it at last," he sighed.

But Mickey was wrong. As soon as his back was turned all the pieces of wood began to move.

Each piece of wood became a new broom. Each new broom grew arms and picked up a bucket in each hand. And they all marched straight towards the fountain to collect water.

Mickey couldn't believe his eyes! He
tried to stop the brooms but they just
knocked him down and walked right
over him.

Like a great army, the brooms kept
marching and marching. They tipped
up their buckets, pouring more and
more water into the overflowing well.

The water in the cellar rose higher and higher. Mickey had to struggle to stay afloat. Then he saw the sorcerer's book of magic spells floating past and jumped onto it.

Quickly, Mickey turned the pages searching for the words that would stop the brooms. He tried very hard to read the words in the book, but it was impossible. The book was being tossed from side to side in the rushing, gushing water.

As Mickey clung onto the book, the water became a mighty, swirling whirlpool. It carried him round and round, faster and faster.

Mickey was terrified!

Luckily, at that very moment, the
sorcerer returned. He knew at once
what his apprentice had done.

Raising his arms, the sorcerer
ordered the water to disappear.

At his command, the water dried up and the brooms and the buckets vanished. Only Mickey's old broom and two buckets remained.

The sorcerer looked down at Mickey with an angry scowl.

Mickey tried to smile as he gave the sorcerer his magic hat. The sorcerer did not smile back at him.

Quickly, Mickey picked up his old buckets and tried to sneak away. But as he went, the sorcerer picked up the broom and gave Mickey's bottom a good, hard *smack!*

Mickey ran off to do his work. He had learned his lesson: never start something that you don't know how to finish!

*　*　*

The music stopped. The audience clapped and cheered. The theatre curtains lowered and the lights brightened.

Suddenly, someone ran out from backstage. It was Mickey Mouse, still wearing his apprentice's robe! He held out his hand to the conductor. "Congratulations, sir," he said.

The conductor shook Mickey's hand. "Congratulations to you, Mickey!" replied the conductor.

"Gee, thanks!" said Mickey, delighted. Everyone had enjoyed a magical time, especially the sorcerer's apprentice – Mickey Mouse!